Fairies of Blossom Bakery

Plum

and the
Winter Ball

Picture Corgi

Acorn
Post Office

Button's House

N

W E

S

Cookie's House

Bubbles
Hair Salon

Elf
Market

Market

Post
Box

Snail
Nail Bar

To little Jasmine Coppard, with love — M.A.
To my mother the constant cake maker — K.H-J.

FAIRIES OF BLOSSOM BAKERY: PLUM AND THE WINTER BALL A PICTURE CORGI BOOK 978 0 552 56902 6 Published in Great Britain by Picture Corgi, an imprint of Random House Children's Publishers UK A Random House Group Company This edition published 2013

1 3 5 7 9 10 8 6 4 2

Copyright © Random House Children's Publishers UK, 2013 Written by Mandy Archer Illustrated by Kirsteen Harris-Jones The right of Mandy Archer and Kirsteen Harris-Jones to be identified as the author and illustrator of this work has been asserted in accordance with the Copyright, Designs and Patents Act 1988. All rights reserved. Picture Corgi Books are published by Random House Children's Publishers UK, 61–63 Uxbridge Road, London W5 5SA
www.randomhousechildrens.co.uk
www.randomhouse.co.uk
Addresses for companies within The Random House Group Limited can be found at: www.randomhouse.co.uk/offices.htm THE RANDOM HOUSE GROUP Limited Reg. No. 954009 A CIP catalogue record for this book is available from the British Library. Printed in Italy

Fairies of Blossom Bakery

Cupcake

Plum

O ver the hills in a land of sweetness,
little fairies bake and play.
Would you like to peep at their secret,
scrumptious world?

Make a wish, then step
into the magic of Fairycake Kingdom
and meet the fairies…

Cookie

Butterfly

Sparkle

Button

Brrr!

It was a fine frosty morning in Fairycake Kingdom. Straight after breakfast, Plum the fairy put on her coat and rushed out to the garden.

"Perfect weather for fruit picking!" she exclaimed. She fluttered happily up and down, filling her basket with juicy berries and plums.

"I'll make a cake and a fruit crumble," she chattered. "Ooh, and a few jars of jam, too!"

The excited fairy reached out to pick a shiny blackberry when **ting!** a tiny white snowflake landed on her nose!

Plum blinked.

"It's the first snowflake of winter," she gasped.

The first snowflake of winter was the start of something special. It began the countdown to the Royal Winter Ball! When Plum arrived to help at the Blossom Bakery Café, all the fairies were talking about it!

"Where will it be?" wondered Button.

"What will we wear?" cooed Butterfly.

Cupcake smiled at her friends.

"Would you put this poster up for me?" she asked Plum.

Plum unrolled a silver sheet of parchment. Sparkle, Cookie, Button and Butterfly all gathered round.

"It's for the Winter Ball," she cried. "It's next Saturday!"

Plum and her friends gazed up at the poster.

You are invited to the
Fairycake Kingdom
Royal Winter Ball

An evening
of music, sparkles
and ice skating

Come to the Seeing Pool
on Saturday
to celebrate the crowning
of the Snow Belle

Please bring something sweet to eat!

"Who will be Snow Belle this year?" whispered Sparkle.

"That's for Princess Crystal to decide," replied Cookie. "The Snow Belle will get to wear her special sparkly tiara!"

"I wish it could be one of us!" gushed Butterfly, fluttering into the air.

Plum didn't even dare to dream of such a thing. Only truly magical fairies were chosen for an honour like that.

It snowed all day and it snowed all night. As if by magic, Fairycake Kingdom turned into a winter wonderland.

"Can't be late!" puffed Plum, bustling along the path as she buttoned up her coat. She had a date to meet her fairy friends at the frozen Seeing Pool.

Whooooooosh! A chilly breeze sent the little fairy's mittens and hat tumbling into the air! She fluttered after them . . . then dropped her skates in the snow.

"How will I ever manage to glide gracefully?" wondered Plum. "I can't even carry my skates properly!"

She picked up her skates and then set off after her mittens and hat.
Too late – the winter wind had already whisked them high above the trees.

"Oh bother," sighed Plum. "Now they're gone for good!"

By the time Plum got to the Seeing Pool, her friends were already pirouetting around the ice. They looked so elegant as they made their twirls and figures of eight.

"Come on!" called Butterfly. "It's heaps of fun!"

Plum laced up her skates, then took a deep breath. Her heart fluttered.

"I'll hold your hand," said Cupcake kindly.

Plum tried her best, but it was hopeless. Every time she took a step, she fell over. Soon her legs ached and her hands felt cold.

"Where are your mittens?" asked Cookie.

"I lost them," said Plum sadly.

Every day there was something new to do for the Royal Winter Ball.
Plum and her friends went to the Elf Market to buy ingredients for their
cakes and bakes.

"I'm bringing gingerbread fairies," said Cookie.

Button turned to Plum. "You must do your scrummy fruit sponge,"
she smiled. "It's perfect for winter weather."

"Shall we go back for tea at the Blossom Bakery Café?" suggested Cupcake.

"Oh yes," nodded Button. "We can talk about the Snow Belle. It's bound to be someone glamorous!"

"I'm afraid I'm busy this afternoon," replied Plum. With a wave and a smile, she fluttered on her way.

Toffee Apples

Lollies

Hot Pies

Pippin's Tasty Treats

Veg

Elf-Made

Back in five mins

Winter Jams

Sugared Plums

As soon as she was out of sight, Plum dashed over to the Seeing Pool.

"A fairy like me has no business daydreaming about the Snow Belle," she sighed. "I can't even skate!"

Plum waited until all the other skaters had gone home. After a while only Nana Puff was left, busy setting up a hot chocolate stall for the Ball.

Slowly and carefully, Plum stepped out on to the shimmering ice.

"I can't give up," she said bravely.

Plum skated all afternoon. The plucky fairy lost count of the times she fell over, but she kept on trying.

"I'm not half as good as my friends," she said quietly, "but I'm getting better."

"Yes, you are!" said a proud voice.

Plum looked up to see Nana Puff beaming back at her!

"You've worked very hard but you look frozen," replied Nana Puff. "Come on, sweetness. Home time."

Plum got up early on Saturday. She had worked late into the night stitching a special dress for the Royal Winter Ball. Now it was just hours away and she was baking her special treat!

"A few more berries and this will be good enough to eat!" She slipped her arm through her basket, then popped outside to pick some.

Chirrp-tiddee-dee!

"Hello to you, too!" smiled Plum, waving to a merry little robin. "Oh my!"

Sunbeams danced across the snowy garden, making it glitter like diamonds. Plum's poor little fingers trembled without any mittens to keep them warm, but she didn't complain.

"This really is my favourite time of year," she sighed happily. She decided to stop and play for a little while.

Plum was still busy making snow fairies when Cupcake peeped over the garden fence.

"Come along, Plum!" she called. "It's time for the Winter Ball!"

"Oh goodness!" gasped Plum. "I forgot the time!"

The flustered fairy darted indoors, leaving a trail of berries behind her.

Cupcake helped her friend put on her shimmering gossamer gown, stitched in delicate layers of silver, purple and blue.

"What a pretty party dress," she exclaimed.

"Thank you," blushed Plum. "I made it myself."

It was time to go.

"I'll just get my tin," said Plum, rushing into the kitchen. She picked it up with both hands, but her fingers were still shivering from the garden. Oh no! The cake slid out of the tin all over her new dress! Poor Plum burst into tears.

"Let's get you changed, then scoop up the cake," suggested Cupcake. "We can sort everything out once we get there. No fairy should be late for the Royal Winter Ball."

As soon as Plum stepped outside, her friends wrapped her in a big fairy hug. "Don't worry about your cake," said Cookie. "It will still taste scrummy." Plum tried to smile, but inside she felt sad. Her cake was ruined, she'd lost her mittens *and* she was a terrible skater!

But when Plum arrived at the Seeing Pool, even she forgot about her rotten luck. The Royal Winter Ball was spectacular!

"Look!" exclaimed Butterfly. "There's Princess Crystal's glittery ice throne."

"Let's put our cakes down," suggested Sparkle.

"Then we can skate!" added Button.

"First things first," said Cupcake, handing Plum a pair of silvery mittens.

Cookie's face lit up. "You can't skate without mittens! We clubbed together to buy you a new pair."

"Thank you!" cried Plum, slipping them on. They fitted perfectly!

Plum still wasn't sure about skating, but she was determined to try her best. "Just take a deep breath," she whispered bravely, lacing up her skates.

The first notes of a beautiful fairy waltz echoed across the Seeing Pool. Plum held out her arms and started to glide.

"I'm dancing on ice!" she laughed, taking in the atmosphere. Soon she was so busy whirling and twirling, she didn't notice her friends bustling round the banqueting table.

Just then, the music stopped.

"It's time to announce the Snow Belle!" said Butterfly in a hushed voice.

"This year's fairy never gives up, even when things are difficult," announced Princess Crystal, winking at Nana Puff "Congratulations, Snow Belle Plum!"

Cheers and whoops echoed across the Seeing Pool. Plum blinked in surprise as her friends helped her make her way up to Princess Crystal.

"You are a truly magical young fairy," smiled Her Majesty, "inside and out!"

"B–b–but my terrible cake . . ." stuttered Plum.

Princess Crystal looked confused.

"It's a baking sensation!" she exclaimed.

Cupcake, Cookie, Button, Sparkle and Butterfly gathered round the banqueting table.

"I don't think the cake was so bad," piped up Cupcake. She lifted up Plum's tin to reveal a stunning upside-down pudding with shimmering fruit on top!

"What happened?" gasped Plum.

"It just needed a sprinkle of winter magic!' whispered Sparkle.

All Plum's dreams had come true. Her hard work had paid off, her cake looked beautiful, and it was all thanks to the magic of fairy friends!

Plum's upside-down pudding

A warming plum and blackberry pudding with a glimmering glaze.

Shopping list for one upside-down pudding

Glaze
- 150g butter
- 75g demerara sugar

Fruit
- 3 ripe plums
- 200g blackberries

Cake Mixture
- 150g plain flour
- 1 large teaspoon baking powder
- Pinch of salt
- 75g butter
- 200g caster sugar
- 1 egg
- 1 teaspoon vanilla essence
- 175ml semi-skimmed milk

1. Ask a grown-up to pre-heat the oven to 180°C/350°F/Gas Mark 4.

2. Tip the butter for the glaze and the demerara sugar into a 23cm round cake tin. Ask your helper to pop the tin into the oven for a few minutes. When the sugar and butter melt together and start to bubble, take the tin out to cool a little.

3. While you wait, you can get the rest of your ingredients ready. Ask a grown-up to help you wash and slice the plums and take out the stones. Wash your blackberries and put them in a colander. Pour the flour, baking powder and salt into a clean bowl and give the mixture a stir.

4. In a large mixing bowl, use a wooden spoon to blend the cake mixture butter with the caster sugar. Crack in the egg and add the vanilla essence.

5. Gradually add a little milk, plus some of the flour mixture. Keep stirring until everything combines. Add the rest of the milk and the flour, bit by bit. When you've got a smooth cake mixture, you're ready to put the pudding together!

6. Ask a grown-up to check that the cake tin is cool enough to touch, then carefully arrange the blackberries and plums around the base. Make sure the whole tin is covered.

Pour in the cake mixture, then ask your helper to pop the tin back in the oven for around 45 minutes.

7. When the pudding looks golden brown, it's ready to take out of the oven. Leave it on the side until it's completely cooled. Now put a plate on the tin and quickly flip it over. Your sponge will have a beautiful caramelized plum and blackberry topping – simply scrumptious!

Fairy Tip
Fairies always wash their hands before starting a new recipe!

Bye-bye for now!

We hope you enjoyed your visit
to the Fairycake Kingdom.

Please join us again for more adventures!